I Married Satan

by

LaDonna M. Smith

I Married Satan

Published by: Fire and Words Publishing™ -a subsidiary of Philatonian Productions™.

Printed in the United States of America.

Cover Designed by: LaDonna M. Smith
Images Courtesy of www.google.com
Edited by: Dr. Arnetha Bowen

www.ladonnamsmith.com

I Married Satan/by LaDonna M. Smith.
Summary: Autobiography of a woman who experiences and yet survives an abusive marriage. 18 years old and older. True-life depiction with the help of:

1. Reality-non fiction
2. Autobiography
3. Biblical references
4. Poetry and song lyrics

Copyright catalog: TXU 1-602-906
ISBN 13: 978-1-4507-2036-6

All scripture references are used with permission in writing from Bud and Bettye Miller from their website: ***http://bibleresources.bible.com.*** *The numeric definitions were based on information found on: http://www.asis.com/users/stag/godcount.html and http://members.cox.net/8thday/meaning.html.*

This book is for every person who has ever been in a relationship with an abusive spouse; or has experienced facets of abuse such as: physical, mental, emotional, spiritual, molestation, drugs, or alcoholism…

You can make it…

I DID.

Thank You To...

First and foremost God, for allowing me to write this book in spite of myself. His son Jesus Christ for dying for my sins and interceding on my behalf. The Holy Spirit for His guidance, comfort, direction, and protection. My mother-Montrue E. Crawford (Nelson) for everything – giving me life and not aborting me. Additionally, for teaching me a lot and providing me with words of encouragement and prayers even when I didn't even pray for myself. My grandfather Edwin Crawford Sr., for filling the void of "*daddy*" and for instilling in me so many words of wisdom, encouragement and guidance. My grandmother Montrue A. Cornish for teaching me a talent that will last a lifetime, and telling me "not to take anything from anybody." My grandparents - Thomas H. Sr. and Gertrude Nelson for completing my family and giving love and support throughout my adolescence and accepting me as your grandchild. My brother Tommy for being my rock. We've been through and overcome a lot together even though you didn't always "want to hear it". My little sister Shanel for holding that special place in my heart and keeping me in line especially when I don't call like I should. My cousin Marcus for being an ear and like a brother to me especially while Tommy was away in Nebraska. My cousin Devon for all of your help and for being like a sister to me...oh and for Jaylen and Amayah. Aunt Martha aka "Girlfriend" for teaching me how to be a lady and not to lie. Not a day goes by that I don't miss you! My Godparents, the late Sebron and Carrie Isom for my first keyboard, love, encouragement, and support. Professor Fred Fair for channeling my energy in the right direction and for reminding me to "*make it happen*" and that "*time is money*". Mrs. Thom for providing me with an alternative and sparking my interest in speech and journalism. My cousin K. Alonzo Hart for "*schooling*" and mentoring me through this entire journey and providing wisdom and "*venting sessions*". Bud and Betty Miller for creating www.bible.com and having it readily available whenever I needed it. Pastor Damien Briggs (Eastern Community Church) for the divine connection and encouragement and "*I'm Praying For Ya's*", Richard, Karen and HannahWyatt (Victory Christian Ministries Int.) for the way you allow God to use you to encourage and fellowship with my "*Mama*" that means a lot to me. Pastor Mark Cloude (New Birth Full Gospel Baptist Church) for speaking this into existence. Pastor Duane and First Lady Miriam Simmons for encouraging me, and being my first "*promoters*". Min. Beverly "*do it*" Johnson and Stevie Johnson for encouraging me to get the book done when I thought about putting it off and second guessed myself. Bishop Marcus A. Johnson and First Lady Ronae Johnson (New Harvest Ministries Int.) –for being my spiritual parents and pushing me in my spiritual growth. My support systems: Annette "*Twin*" Shelton, Ricky "*The King*" Hart Jr., B. Bladen "*Stew*" Stewart, Mary "*Girl You is Crazy*" Herndon, Sean "*My Brother*" McCoy, Uncle David "*I Love My Niece*" Smith, Greg "Money-G" McKeaver, Paul "*I Love You Cuz*" Ferguson, Greg "*Coogi*" Campbell, and Mike "*Mike Nyce*" Middleton, Warren "*I hope THIS Makes You Smile*" Decatur for mentoring me. I can never repay your for pushing the business *SHE-E-Oh!* in me.

You have each come at different points and times in my life; encouraged me, motivated me, talked to me and have been there when I needed you, even times- when you didn't know.

To anyone else who thought I should have listed your name above, please place it here

_________________________________.

To each one of you **I Love You**!

WARNING and DISCLAIMER

Please be advised that names have been changed in an effort to protect the identities of the involved persons.

Mainly because knowing what I do know of him, he would still probably try to do something crazy in an effort to hurt me and attack me. Unfortunately, he would think that I wrote this book for and will be getting lots of money instead of ministry and help.

FYI: I wrote this as therapy for me to begin the healing process.

Please know that without a shadow of doubt that Satan has no authority anymore in my life spiritually, physically or mentally. He tries, but God already established a hedge of protection.

My mom told the man I thought that I had married a long time ago that no weapon formed against me or my family would prosper. I mean you/it formed but you/it didn't prosper.

He may have beaten the legal system but he can't beat God.

After reading this book some people may feel that it isn't very "God like". However, there is one thing that you have to remember. Although I had accepted Jesus Christ into my life, I hadn't developed a relationship with him. So during this time of my life I wasn't living in a *Godly* way. The book is not endorsing my behavior – it is simply revealing my actions and behaviors behind the mask of "churchy-ness". There are a lot of people who come to church and know how to perpetrate what to wear, how to talk, when to praise dance etc. but are simply masking hurt, pain, emotions and issues.

I have personally decided to be transparent in this book because I have learned from experience that this was my season to have experiences that would play vital roles in my purpose for my life.

How can someone speak from experience – without going through the experience? If someone comes to you –you can only give them an opinion not advice!

This book is simply a reflecting pool to those who are or have been in similar situations.

To You from ME…

To you from me I give you strength to overcome and
the power and victory to get through the situation
I give you mercy and forgiveness to show you
that I have never left you nor forsaken you.

I empower you with knowledge and wisdom
to make the right decisions and follow…
The proper pathways and procedures to success.
For I have already told you that your enemies would be stools…
for your feet.

If you act in humbleness and only stand still
you will be the head and not the tail,
First not the last
and my glory shall be revealed.

Why do you wallow and dwell…
on the situations you already overcame?
When I have given you all of the tools of success…so move on
Stop think and tap into the power
I gave to you before you were even born.

Just know that I allowed this to occur to grow and mature you
So that you can help the next person I send your way
and so that you will know and appreciate me.
From me to you in your life I give you ME.

-Love God

through LaDonna M. Smith

The Agenda

Extras

Preface

Maybe it was because I was sexually abused from at least the age of fourteen and down through my younger years (the earliest I remember is five) by not one but five different people who were supposed to be looked at as family (it is a secret that will be taken to my grave if I haven't already told you); or maybe because I felt unloved and wanted attention. Maybe because I didn't feel good about myself because I was told that I looked like a duck and called butter ball when I hit puberty and started developing breast, hips and a big butt; Maybe it was because I watched my grandfather get so drunk that he would fall down the steps (thank God he got delivered from alcohol a demon that played all sides of my family-yep a generational curse). Or maybe because I had created jealousy of my little brother because he always got the new in style clothes and I always had to share my clothes with my mother (until I got old enough to buy them for myself); Maybe it was because I was always being compared to other cousins and had to share barrettes and hair do's. Maybe it was just because I had to take a bath in the same bath water that my mother did right after she got out of the tub; Or maybe it was because I felt that my mother hated the fact that I was born, ruined her life and caused her to miss out on so much of her own life; Maybe it was because I always felt like I was just taking up space in this world since I always felt like a second class citizen squatting; or maybe because I cried myself to sleep and contemplated suicide only for my brother to talk me out of OD'n on pills and/or slitting my wrist; Maybe it was just because my father never came around and didn't want me; and my stepfather physically abused my mother, eventually giving me my first black eye and nose bleed; Or just maybe because the guy who I gave my virginity to (*not really even knowing I was a virgin or how to be one because of the sexual abuse*), made me feel embarrassed because he said that I was "*tight*", and not in the good slang way.

Whatever it was… When I jumped into getting married I saw it as a way of escape, yet I didn't realize how serious of a situation I was getting into. I had gotten married when I shouldn't have…too soon and not in God's biblical order for my life. Although, if I hadn't, I may not have written this book, gained a real testimony, or learned my purpose in life.

From the verbal, mental, emotional, spiritual, and physical abuse, I became an even more damaged woman. The devil had already left his bags in my life and I suppressed issues. Issues that would mess up just about every romantic relationship that I would have, cause me to attract the wrong type of man *to* me, and settle for them and their issues.

I had become a woman who became afraid to be alone because of the dependency developed by my ex __________ (husband, supposed to be husband, thought to be husband –you fill in the blanks).

It scared off guys no matter how good or bad for me they were. Tyler Perry said it best-"some people are in your life for a season and some for a lifetime". I sometimes wonder how many potential lifetimes, I had pushed away and conversely how many seasons I kept around way too long.

I had people at churches where I attended ignore situations at hand, and even my family thought that I was the CRAZY one in my marriage. The more I cried out, the more the devil had pulled the covers over their eyes-everyone's eyes-even mine and pretty much caused me to want to leave this world sooner than God had planned for me to- again.

I once heard someone say that the devil will use someone close to you to hurt you…and that's what I always found to be true. The more I thought about it, the more I had to get my mind reconditioned. I had to work harder than most not to totally lose my mind.

Thanks be to God who had my life's purpose in His hands and gave me time to realize Him and His purpose for me. I see now that I had to go through an abusive marriage and the situations that occurred from it because of all of the people God has sent my way since this has happened. I was like the woman in the Bible who had the issue of blood and had to press her way through a crowd of people to see Jesus. My blood issue was life and my crowd was life's circumstances. Yet, Jesus was there all along and welcomed me into His loving arms, time and time again.

WOW! Over a four and a half year time span, I had been homeless, evicted from almost every residence I had called home --three different places,; used for the little bit of money that I did come across; hungry; smoking cigarettes and "blacks", weed, and drinking; felt lonely and like I didn't fit in; I contemplated suicide; I was depressed, felt worthless; disrespected, angry, violent, desperate, called vulnerable and gullible I experienced three house raids within six months in 2005 (still not totally sure why). I had to deal with shyster types of landlords, lost two cars, been in debt, been to visit people in and out of prisons, cried off and on, I felt like I was in a whirlwind. I came within feet of a dead body just off the machines in the hospital not in a casket and I lived in a house with not one but two cremated bodies in a box. I attracted men who really didn't care about me and often lied saying that they loved and cared about me and to top it all off, I was unattached from a church so I church *hop'd* and I could say so much more but…

Just to become a completely whole woman now….

Thank you God!

Chapter I

Colossians 3:1-5

Since then you have been raised with Christ, set your hearts on things above, where Christ is seated at the right hand of God. Set your minds on things above, not on earthly things. For you died, and your life is now hidden with Christ, in God. When Christ, who is your life appears, then you also will appear with Him in glory. Put to death therefore whatever belongs to your earthly nature, sexual immorality, impurity, lust, evil desires, and greed, which is idolatry.

LaDonna M. Smith

>WHEN TROUBLE MET VEE<

I decided that my biological clock was ticking and that it was time to settle down and get married. Especially since all of my other cousins around my age had already gotten married and/or had children, so what was I waiting for? I was twenty-five years old.

Earlier that year, I had caught the bouquet at my cousin's wedding. This is symbolic because in traditional American wedding ceremonies, if an unmarried female catches the bride's bouquet, she is the next bride to be. In keeping with superstition, my time had to be near.

I got married that August…or so I thought…

The story of my "marriage" began when my neighbor died... I was asked to play the piano/organ for her funeral to be held at the church where my grandfather had us so actively involved, as children. I was an acolyte, attended Sunday school, and was once, the church musician; and my mom was the choir director and trustee. .

We were raised in that church, literally. Everyone who attended that church knew the Crawford family. My Great-Grandparents had attended that church; my grandparents and mother had gotten married in that church. I had been a musician there, even though it wasn't the first church where I played the piano. .

Attending this Methodist church allowed me to have friends in high school and in the neighborhood. When we were there…well let's just compare it to a certain movie about a church's transformation from being "dead" and having hardly any members to a good crowd every Sunday.

Anyway, I remember my neighbor as a quiet lady in the later years of her life. She had earned the right to be quiet, in my opinion, living to be over one hundred.

And growing up she was always nicely dressed and was outspoken in church---she was even a math whiz. My grandfather used to tell my brother and me to "go ask Ms. G" for help with my homework since she used to be a schoolteacher and a trustee at church. Her house was huge with a huge yard and she never had any children or a husband.

She always remembered our birthdays and we knew that on our birthdays and any other special occasions, as well as coming outside to watch me leave for my prom. We could always expect a present from the house next door – *Her house.*

Most of the time (and as far I can remember) we always got a greeting card with money in it. So being asked to play for her funeral service was expected, especially since it appeared that I was the neighborhood musician other than my cousin who also played and later re-became a member of the church. Besides Ms. G's niece offered me fifty dollars to play for the service, at a time when I was working two part time jobs and in school. Cool, or so I thought. Any and every little penny helped, even though my mom always taught me not to play for money. But a *sistah* needed that little bit of change.

After I played for the funeral, we went to the repast at the church. Later, her niece asked me to come over to Ms. G's house to get my stipend. I really didn't want to go but my mother convinced me that we should. I felt weird going over to and being in that house, knowing that Ms. G had died and in that house. I felt that it was going to be a *spooky* ...and it was.

>THE ARRIVAL<

Well I did go, but we first pulled into my grandfather's driveway. As we pulled in, I noticed that there was a green truck in the driveway and a man taking a child out of a car seat from the back seat.

He was tall, dark and handsome the way that I like - no love my man. I always wanted to date someone with a truck so…so far two for two. The only thing that seemed to be wrong about him was that he had a child – or so I thought.

I flirted and talked trash about him parking in my grandfather's-- no my yard-- and in my parking space—you know I had to hype it up! And he politely entertained it. I mean, the only reason that I said something in the first place was because his family was always so quick to trip or say something to allude to the fact that no other vehicles except there's was to park in the space - when we or someone else parked on their side of the parking space.

See, we had a parking space that was on inside part of our yard; but they had parking spaces on both the inside and outside parts of their yard. Their exterior parking space was right next to our yard and looked as if it could have been part of our yard if there hadn't been a fence to separate the yards. My mother knows me as being one who is very straight forward and bold and one who has no problem speaking before she thinks--proceeded to take me inside of our neighbor's house and cut the "smart" flirtatious comments short.

>WOLF IN SHEEP'S CLOTHING<

We walked in and sat on the couch after speaking to the people who my mom already knew, and who throughout the day I had grown to know.

"Hey V" rang as he came through the door. And I looked up at this wolf in sheep's clothes that I saw as a potential challenge to get. I was on a mission. And although the bible says in *Proverbs 18:22 He that findeth a wife, findeth a good thing*...I found him and he was my target.

I was desperate and I didn't have a boyfriend. He looked like a good prospect with great potential. I had NO *cut* cards.

>OUT WITH THE OLD AND IN WITH THE NEW<
A FLASHBACK

I had recently ended a relationship with a guy who was a little older than me, and whom I had met in a nightclub's detoxification area, where he worked as a bouncer.

My girls and I had gone to the club to celebrate the Pisces' birthdays in our friendship circle. We were on the stage in the VIP section of the club and I had gotten very drunk, and felt lightheaded. The room had begun to spin. We were on the stage in VIP. I am still not one hundred percent sure on how we got in VIP. The only explanation that I have is that we got there for dirty dancing.

I went into the bathroom to cool off, and I threw up. But

I had enough sense to know that I didn't want to touch the seat or "hug the toilet".

Anyway, the guy was kinda built; dark skinned, tall, with a baldhead, and in my opinion (maybe because I was drunk) very sexy. *Recap-me and the girls had gone out collectively on a ladies night to celebrate the March birthdays in VIP and somehow I ended up drinking something that caused me to lean my body on the speaker, needing some air and feeling nauseous and before I knew I, be in the bathroom trying to lean over the urine covered seat to throw up.* Ewwww....I prayed that the stuff didn't splash on me or the seat. It was so nasty! All I wanted to do was sit down, but the "bouncer" who was working the floor, told me that I couldn't sit on the steps right outside of the bathroom.The only option that I had to feel better, without leaving the club and ruining the night for my friends, was to go to the Detox Room and he personally escorted me.

But once I got down there, my visit to the room wasn't that bad. The first person I met was Richard. After we conversed briefly, I asked him to get my friends from the upstairs – dance floor area of the club so that we could all be together. He did, and instead of me recuperating (since I was the driver) we were downstairs in the room laughing at everyone else throwing up and falling all over the place. People were literally losing control of their bodily functions and actions.We were doing well – that is until he started staying away and I met "Vee". So Vee was really a rebound relationship.

>GETTING BACK TO THE POINT<

Ok…so back to the story of me meeting "Vee".

Before long I could tell that he had taken interest in me as well. He and I began going back in forth comparing, and bragging about the materialistic things that we owned, in addition to who we were. I had a college degree - he had a college degree; I had my own car - he had two trucks and a minivan; I lived with my Momma-he had his own house; I had my own business - he had his own business; neither one of us had kids…and well...it seemed like we had finally met our match.

Everyone said it.

It is unfortunate that I had been so open and honest about myself. Later I found out that over sixty percent of the things Vee had said were false-yep all lies.

James 1:19 says: *My dear brothers take note of this: Everyone should be quick to listen, slow to speak and slow to become angry.*

But that didn't stop the house from being silent and the heads going back and forth during our "rounds" of battle. It was as if the entire conversation had been scripted and rehearsed.

Eventually we left without exchanging phone numbers, or did I give him my phone number? Oh yea, I gave him mine, because he wanted me to speak to some youths that he claimed that he worked with at a church or something. Yet and still another lie. I later found out that he hadn't been to church in God knows how long. Whatever…for some reason I just wanted to talk to him some more. Let's be real, I was turned on by the person that I thought that he was. At that time in my life, I was materialistic and a gold digger.

About a week later, I still hadn't heard from him. Who did he think he was not to contact me – me of all people? Being bold, and having enough of the indirect rejection, I stopped back over his grandmother's house.

"By chance, did Vee leave his business card for me?" I asked since that is what we had planned on him doing.

To my surprise, he had done just that.

>THE CHASE IS ON<

As I was making the fifteen-minute drive back home, I called him and we talked. Soon after our conversation began, we planned a date. Yes, I know, I broke every rule in dating I had begun to create - like let the man chase you, you never call the same day, if he doesn't call - oh well it wasn't meant to be etc. etc. etc. But I was determined to get this man. Our first date was going to start late because he had to work and wasn't getting off until about 10:00 pm. Really… he wasn't…but that is what he said. We had planned to go bowling, but instead just drove around and talked since the bowling alley and everything was closed. My gut feeling made me start thinking and I started asking questions. When I did, I found out that he had a live in girlfriend. I didn't care because I was confident that I could steal him from her. My arrogance and confidence was at a peak, and I wanted this good man, because he had everything I wanted and needed and was going to be mine! I was going to have him. Obviously, she wasn't woman enough to be with a man like this. And he was there now with me.

>TELEPHONE LINE<

From that day on Vee and I talked everyday - all day. He even began popping up at my mom's house to get hugs, just to see me and spend time with me. Especially, after we had sex for the first time.

I have to admit I was getting ready to come on my menstrual cycle and extremely horny, (aka being in the mood) For me, being close to that time of the month always got me in trouble and beds. That is how I ended up conceiving my child; Thanksgiving 1997 and the abortion occurred February 1998. It's a shame that my child's father and I are no longer close. We used to be best friends who could talk about everything and did

---

about anything. In case he does read this – yes I still love you! When we were in my bed, Vee said that he didn't want to do it so soon in our relationship. But since it had happened -it was ok. He knew that it was good and that he enjoyed it. That was my way of sealing the deal on "operation gotta get married soon".

>OBSESSIVE<

I later found out that his wanting to see and be with me all the time was a bad thing - a controlling thing. I don't think that it was even a month later that he had put the live in girlfriend out of the house, after she left for work, by changing the locks, and I had moved in. The time had come when I had begun to spend the night over his house and he would meet me at work to make sure that I got home safely. Well… to his house safely. He liked me so much that he wanted to be with me as much as he could– every wakening minute. Really he saw a meal ticket with me working two jobs, and having a television show. And I think he could sense my emotional damage. During that time, I thought that I could trust him with knowing intricate details about my past. You know things that people discuss in relationships: like past lovers, past friends, past sexual experiences and more. But little did I know that he would later use the information that he got from me against me and to my disadvantage. Things that were supposed to be covered by him – for me - from the world – intimate moments that I disclosed to him in the privacy of our home - the home - which *we* were starting to build. He now had someone who cooked for him and cleaned for him and sexed him as much as he wanted, and he had it better than good. I thought that I had it good too…since I was no longer living in my Momma's house at twenty-five, I had my car, a house, and a MAN. I was practicing being married, and I wanted to show Vee that I was definitely *wifey* material. I settled for him and despite the God in me telling me that shacking and fornicating was wrong; I was going to make everything right by getting Vee to marry me.

>GROSS<

Everything was perfect…that is from May 2003-until July 2003. The funeral of Ms. G was in April, but little did I know the devil was already planning my funeral. Things really started getting crazy when the ex-girlfriend popped up over to the house one day and demanded that Vee open the door so that she could get her things. Vee would not open the door and only talked to her through the door. As she begged relentlessly for her belongings and most importantly her cosmetology license, he boldly lied and said that he didn't have it or her things. I didn't realize that I was watching an episode of *V-TV*-a reality show, that I would eventually be cast as the main character. However, there was a slight variation to the story and the main character- he married me.

When Vee's ex had knocked on the door, he was actually sitting on the toilet. I know for a fact that he jumped up off of it very quickly and didn't have time to wipe his butt. He just pulled up his pants. *Ewwww.* And the worst part was that he was *ok* with his actions. As soon as she left, he returned to the toilet to finish his business…

Chapter II

>LIVING COLORS OF LOVE<

By the fourth week of being married to Vee, I started to see a change. The man, who had once showed so much love and compassion to me, had begun to be cold and heartless. I was beginning to be verbally and mentally abused, and taken for granted.

I remember a time when I had a job at a temp agency and it was going well. They had moved me to the front desk and I truly believe that I was on my way to becoming a permanent employee at the main local office. That was until Vee decided that he was going to start revealing his true colors. Vee began to call my job constantly and obviously not caring about jeopardizing my job due to the frequency of his calls. I had seen signs before when he called me at the amusement park, but what was really happening didn't "click" in my head. I was in love with a fantasy.

>LUNCH BREAK<

I was sitting at work one day and I decided to take lunch a little earlier than usual. As I think back it had to be God speaking through the Holy Spirit. My car note had fallen so far behind that the lender was trying to find my car to repossess it. *On a side note, I thought both car notes and all of our bills were being paid by Vee since he was in charge of our finances. Vee knew that.* I walked out the door of the office and I know that it had to be God and the Holy Spirit to have me walk next door to the bank to withdraw money from my account that Vee had me add him onto. I was not *allowed* to be added to his but he HAD to be on my accounts and have access to my accounts. I walked over to the ATM machine at a bank beside where I was working but then for some reason, I changed my mind walked over to my car. As soon as I turned the corner whom did I see getting out of their truck and getting into my car...? He had already taken my keys to his vehicles but he sure enough had and was about to use the one he had for my car. Vee was planning to take my car to make me think that the repo man had come and gotten it. We began to argue and I walked off towards the place I was about to walk to for lunch.

>LUNCH TKO<

Lunch was being bought for my boss and me. Actually I was going to lunch and I had asked her if she wanted me to bring her back something and she gave me money. Vee followed me to the restaurant and asked if he could talk to me. We sat in the restaurant eating and I really didn't have anything to say to him because of what he had just attempted to do. Then he did the unimaginable and unexpected. Vee snatched my wallet and ATM card and went to an ATM and withdrew a hundred dollars. A hundred dollars may not seem like a lot of money but to someone who was barely maintaining a lifestyle on a Temporary Associate's paycheck of about $12.00 per hour – it was a lot of money. He was my husband all he really had to do was ask for it – ok, not really, but he stole it! There are two types of people that I try my best not to associate with - liars and thieves - and he proved to be both. He had an ATM card for my/our account but he wanted to cover his behind and he knew that I had no leg to stand on if he used my card and because he knew my pin code to the account. There was nothing I could do he had taken the money. He said he did it because I was not paying bills. Not totally true. Actually if he didn't keep taking my money I could have helped him more. I did what I first thought to do since I had no money on me. I dialed 911 and they told me that there was nothing that they could do since he had access to the account and HE *WAS* MY HUSBAND. As I walked back to work disgusted, he came out of nowhere in his truck and then somehow on foot. I started walking back to work faster and Vee walked up to me, I sat my boss' food on a step to entertain and go back and forth with Vee. I stooped down to his level. Then out of anger and pure spite, Vee knocked my boss' food to the ground. I nervously tried to walk back to work trying to think of how I was going to explain to my boss what had just happened. I began to explain to my boss speaking generally and playing it off like it was no big deal while discretely asking for help as I tried to protect myself from being embarrassed. Vee followed me to the back office break room/supply room area - an area off limits to the general public. Afraid that I was about to lose my job I declared to my boss that I was going to have to leave work for the day. I couldn't concentrate and I apologized for the lunch situation. Vee boldly told her that he had knocked it down and that he would reimburse her. I knew that Vee wasn't going to leave that day peacefully and without a scene. So, I left my job to protect the safety of the other two employees-my bosses. I went home and the argument continued.

>BACK ON CAMPUS<

Despite me not losing my job at the temp agency, I was totally humiliated. I was ecstatic when I got the call from Prince George's Community College saying that I could start a temp job with them in a Dean's Office. This would be my first government job on any level and would give me a chance to save what little bit of dignity I had left. In essence, this would be a true attempt to rid my embarrassment from the incidents that occurred while working at the temp agency, and hopefully preserve the safety of those who worked at the temp agency with me. I just knew in my mind, that there was no way that Vee would be able to do anything to me or my job on campus. Boy was I wrong - again.

>NEW OFFICE<

A permanent position in the Dean's Office had been posted on the job's bulletin board, at the college. Since I was already working in the position, I was given an opportunity to interview for the position. And despite me having the necessary qualifications, as well as the experience needed for the position, I did not get the job. I didn't get the job because I didn't qualify, I didn't get it because Vee had already started calling constantly and coming to the office and making a scene, which scared my bosses and coworkers. Once someone else who transferred from another department filled that position, I was offered a full time job in another department. I was only making about twenty one thousand dollars a year but the job was doing well. That is until Vee started his cycle of calling, coming to the office, harassing and attempting to make me lose my job. Vee called compulsively for many days and in one day in particular as much as seventy-six times. I had become very stressed out and my attendance was becoming affected. Between the tons of IMs and phone calls (same M.O. as when he called me at my other jobs - couldn't reach me-go through the main switchboard etc), I was performing my job duties horribly. No one cared about my personal situations or what was going on, so I figured that it would be better for me to resign from my position, instead of being fired.

>OVER THE RIVER AND THROUGH THE WOODS<

By this time, I had already moved to Baltimore and the commute was really driving me crazy. I caught the MTA bus at 5:20 a.m. so that I could get to the Marc commuter train station every morning by 6:20 a.m., then run to the end of the bus terminal to take the County Bus called “The Bus”, and make it to work by 8:00 a.m. Then in the evening to get back home, I would have to catch “The Bus” at the college at 4:15 p.m., then the 4:40 p.m. MARC commuter train, and catch another MTA bus, which got me home around 6:00 p.m. This commute was costing me around $16.00 for a weekly bus pass and seven dollars each way daily on the train. Here is a secret I had learned and practiced-if you caught the right car in the evening back-you could ride for free, especially if you make friends with the right conductor (but keep that between you and me).

So I was able to save some money.

>MORE MONEY, MORE PROBLEMS<

Eventually, I had found a job in Baltimore, which paid four thousand dollars more than the college so I jumped on it quickly. It was time. I had reported the harassing calls to campus police and Vee was banned from campus until I left. Besides, Vee and the commute were draining my body, making me tired and unproductive. On a side note, I found out some more truths about Vee's past.

>UNTOLD STORIES<

First, I found out that Vee had gotten put out of the military because he was diagnosed as being bipolar and as having *hammer toes* (just another thing which contributed to him not liking himself). He had also gotten in trouble for putting his hands on a female spouse. Yep, a domestic violence charge. Vee told me that this happened because she had taken his keys and he touched her hand, as he grabbed them back. Now, I can understand being falsely accused, and you never repeating the actions. But as you will see this false accusation became all too familiar to me as he did the same thing to me.The difference is that Vee always tried to take my keys from me. I also got put outside of the house a couple of times including in the winter in just a t-shirt and a pair of socks. Still to this day have a bruise on my foot from Vee taking my keys and reacting towards me attempting to retrieve my belongings from *his* truck.

So I guess if he had been permitted to stay in the military while he was married to me, then he would have eventually gotten *kicked* out for being a domestic violence offender anyway…

>MONEY IN THE BANK<

And even more vital, I found out that all of that time

Vee had my paychecks going into his bank account, I could have opened my own account through the credit union that he was a member of through the military, regardless of my personal financial difficulties. Because I was his spouse, I automatically qualified.

>COME STRAIGHT HOME<

I was a missing out on blessing and people begin to start to stay away from me. Even on the college campus –my Alma Mata-where a lot of people knew me. Since I got off of work at 4:00 pm and only worked 10-15 minutes from the house I had to be home in exactly 10-15 minutes. If I got home any later I was automatically accused of cheating, sleeping around and being on a date. Ultimately, all hell would break loose.

>LUNCHTIME<

There was a time when a co-worker had come to my office and asked me if I wanted him to pick me something up for lunch. I was giving him money although with a lot of my true friends I didn't have to. Vee over heard the conversation and conjured up in his mind that I was going on a lunch date, with the man. What he should have worried about was the "lunch dates" and discrete encounters that I started having in my office, once he started treating me horribly and I felt worthless. Especially when most of the school's department was gone from the building during session breaks. I had lost my self-respect and self-worth.

Oh yea about that coworker who was getting me lunch that day, we did later have sex two times on campus. One time in the office across from mine and the second time was in a building being renovated and we finished just in time, because someone came in just as we had gotten dressed. How exciting. Then things go weird and creepy. He started hanging around my office off and on for numerous hours a day. At least until people who worked in my department started complaining? He may have really had feelings for me. But my feelings were purely lust not love.

There was another guy who tried to be my pimp and get me to have sex with men for money and give him a portion of it. I really needed the money and it sounded good. Although I had taken his offer into consideration and came close to taking him up on it, the Holy Spirit in me wouldn't let me do it, and I decided against it. The attention of other men was becoming my drug of choice, because I used to be the person who had lots of friends and family support. Now I was becoming alone even with Vee in the house. Vee was a mason and he would go to Masonic meetings and Masonic functions but I was never invited to any of the social events or permitted to go out, with or without him. Some people may argue that Vee was justified in his insecurities and the men around me. But really he wasn't. Because Vee accused me so many times of doing things that I wasn't doing - I eventually bowed down to the temptations of other men.

>SERVICE<

While working on campus in an office, Vee had me served at work by a sheriff accusing me of second-degree assault against him.

He had filed the charges because I had filed a protective order against him for assaulting me. This was humiliating and more of a reason to leave the campus and yet another job.

Chapter III

>DAY OF THANKS<

Thanksgiving is supposed to be a day to spend with family and friends and to give thanks for all that God has given and done for us…

Vee and I had started visiting different churches so I thought that the devil was just starting to attack us because of that.

Our relationship had really begun to be tenser.

>LOVE TAPS ON THANKSGIVING MORNING<

That morning my cousin called and asked if I could pick him up from BWI airport. Vee and I took a trip to the airport. As I drove back from the airport Vee and I were playing and laughing in the front seats of the car exchanging what I thought were little *love taps*. When we got to the house we were still putting on a front for my cousin of OK’ness, in our relationship. Eventually we began to argue and exchange words and things quickly got out of hand and totally out of control. Vee couldn’t look like less of a man or like I was dominating him, so things began to escalate and get worse and worse. It was getting close to the time that we were to leave to go to my Uncle's house for Thanksgiving dinner. Vee kept blocking the doorway into the bathrooms as I tried to get dressed, so that we could leave to go to my uncle’s house for the family’s thanksgiving dinner. After the arguing began, I tried to be passive and quickly get dressed. I was only wearing my bra and underwear when I went into the hallway bathroom to put on deodorant and to do my hair. Vee was still determined to tell me a piece of his mind.

>SNAP<

I was fed up with Vee picking on me and following me around harassing me. Eventually, enough was enough and without even thinking, I pushed Vee out of my way. In retaliation he put his finger or hand in my face, which really set me off. Months of anger and abuse became surfaced, mixed with boldness, since my cousin was downstairs. I snapped and I hit him. Vee retaliated by hitting me back causing me to fall on the floor crying, and holding my face in disbelief. As I lay there, Vee yelled downstairs to my cousin that my cousin had better come upstairs and get me. My cousin didn't want to see me half dressed and he wasn't supposed to. Truthfully my cousin was half drunk so he really didn't comprehend what was going on. Why didn't he kick Vee's tail for hitting me? Even when he sobered up? I was expecting a different reaction. Both were in the military and learned the same tactics of fighting. My cousin should have at least combined that with anger and prior knowledge of martial arts... or at least confronted Vee. Honestly, I don't know if I was afraid because Vee had hit me or because what may transpire later between Vee and me.

>HOLY GHOST BOLDNESS<

I remember calling my mother to tell her "*I was going to be late or not going to be able to make it"*. She kept asking what was wrong. The more that I tried to conceal the fact that I was crying she could hear the cry for help in my voice. My mother is my mother, and I knew that she would pick up on what was going on. She did just that - read between the lines. Vee picked up another phone and tried to talk over me as he pleaded his case with my mother as I tried to tell her what was going on. She wasn't buying his story and calmly said, "*I'm on my way*". Within minutes my mother and brother came from my uncle's house. *"Vee I told you not to hit my daughter again didn't, I or else you would have to deal with me"*, she said repeatedly. To be honest, I have to give it to my mom; she was in Vee's face. I was proud that my mother was so bold, and I wish at that time –sooner rather than later - that I had that same boldness. But I wasn't because Vee had torn me down and made me feel inadequate, insecure, unconfident, scared and just plain low. The only things that Vee could do were apologize and call my mother "*Ma*". I just kept remembering thinking that that was my mother not his. My mother encouraged me to get dressed and go over to my Uncle's house as planned because I needed to be around family. So I got dressed and although we rode separately all of us including Vee went. When we got over my uncle's house, my uncle told Vee that he wanted to talk to him. I don't know what exactly what was said, but everything seemed to be OK when we left.

>KISS UP<

In an effort to gain my mother's trust in him again, Vee and I went to her church the Sunday after thanksgiving. As soon as the invitation to join the church was extended to the church, Vee got up out of his seat went up front to join/accept it. Thinking that we needed to join a church together as husband and wife, I followed him, hoping that this initiative would cause a change in our relationship and lives. Vee had been raised in a Lutheran Church and I had accepted Christ as my Lord and Savior and been baptized twelve years prior to us joining my mom's church. I went in the back for prayer for those of us who had joined under Christian experience. While in there I asked for prayer from a woman who was married, because I thought that I would be able to gain strength and encouragement from her.

>FUNKY PRAYER<

The lady asked me what I needed prayer for specifically odd but I told her. I pulled back the hair that was covering my black eye that Vee had given me 3 days prior, and all she said was "*ok*".

No - *who did this*? *What happened*? Or any other type of compassion? Probably, because I have gone through my marital situation, I recognize some of the signs of an abusive relationship. She may have been in an abusive relationship as well.

>MINT<

As the lady whispered a prayer, I was distracted. I have to admit that I really didn't concentrate on her prayer or the words that she was saying, and therefore I couldn't come into agreement with what she was praying, because she had the worse breath in the world to me.

>THE AFTERMATH<

After service, I rode home with a different towards my husband. Not because of the prayer, but because of being with God-somewhat. During the service I was afraid to praise and worship for real because I felt that if I did too much Vee would get angered and would make me suffer the consequences and repercussions later for letting everyone know that something was going on. I thought that this meant that our lives were getting ready to change, and that I would finally be safe from Vee's wrath. But I was wrong --it worsened.

>QUICK BIBLE LESSON<

Why would I think that the devil would leave me alone and allow me to get to my destiny? I hadn't learned my purpose in life yet. I was married to Vee, and the devil definitely didn't want to look good in God's sight. Remember the devil did get kicked out of Heaven and told God that he would show God that us humans were bad, and that he was better than us. Vee always tried to show everyone, especially at church, that I was bad and that he was better than me…coincidence? No, I had married Satan. Not the image that many people had about a man in a red suit, with a pointy tail. Running around with a pitchfork. But any person who allows the devil to use him to do satanic acts like lying, killing and destroying. God has given us all a choice. When we make the choice to do wrong, we serve the devil and he is our ruler. Don't allow the devil to use you.The devil is a spirit and the captain of an army seeking to destroy all human beings' chance of spending an everlasting life with God in Heaven; like we are supposed to once we die. He wants us to spend in eternity being tormented in hell by enslaving us in sin. If we allow him to manifest sin in our lives - sin will be manifested. If we don't we will prosper as God has destined us to do.

>Three Gifts...Three Occasions<

I received gifts from Vee on three occasions: Christmas 2003, Valentine 's Day 2004, and March 15, 2004-my birthday.

>CHRISTMAS<

Around Christmas, we had gone to NY to go shopping with my cousin and her husband. Vee and I argued just about the entire trip, causing even more embarrassment. Although, I did buy two pairs of shoes and some purses and perfumes from Canal Street-Vee kept most of it after I left him for the final time. Anyway, my Christmas gifts from Vee were horrible. He had gotten me some aromatherapy candles (some were broken and had to be returned), a day at the spa and the ugliest black and white dress bought a size too small. The dress was an old school one piece with solid black on the top and white at the bottom. It looked like something off an old movie whereas an old lady with a bunch of cats would wear as her *good* clothes. Because it was twenty-five stages past ugly and too small, I never wore the dress. Vee brought all of my gifts off of a home shopping network and I had bought him a suit with the accessories. I was disappointed in all of the gifts that Vee had given me except for the spa.

>THE SPA<

Months later, I went to the spa for the first time in my life, was pampered, and had a massage, - and… yep you guessed it. When I got home, I was accused of sleeping with the massage therapist.

Roger, the massage therapist was sexy as I don't know what, and I know a lot of women had to have asked for him when they came into the spa. I felt high (intoxicated) after he touched me from head to toe for an hour. And I remember getting "moist" from his touch and wanting him to *take* me and have sex with me, right there on the table. I didn't care about Vee or what was going on. I felt that he wanted me as much as I wanted him. But he behaved. Roger later explained that he wanted me too… but couldn't because the door wasn't locked and someone could have walked in at any time. He would have gotten in a lot of trouble and possibly fired. He just didn't understand how much I needed him.

>HOUSE PARTY<

I thought it was *ok* to share with Vee the fact that I had gotten Rogers' number so that I could throw a girl's day party at our house (partial truth and not the complete truth so help me God). The plan was to have massages in one room, passionate (sex) toys in another room, jewelry in another and a clothing swap. It was the perfect idea…*Ruined*! Vee took the entire idea to another level and ultimately ruined it. He called Roger and told him off about wanting to sleep with me. Soon Roger stopped calling me and eventually we lost contact. That was until I saw him on campus later. The bottom line is although I never did have that get together for the girls, when I did talk to Roger I was able to explain to him what was happening and why. He and I briefly hooked up in my office…temporarily Roger was mine. But only once.

>CHRISTMAS PARTY AT VEE's (JOB)<

Vee came dressed in a white tuxedo jacket, to a Christmas party at his job. What a 'bama'. He looked like he was the servant instead of an invited guest and he was mocked. People were looking at him strangely and comments were made. My outfit was cute, appropriate and served the purpose. I wore a nice red scoop neck blouse, a black and white skirt, black tights and some red shoes. I was surprised that I was even invited. But this was how everyone would know that he did in fact have a wife. His mother and other family didn't want to have anything to do with him, except for when they had to, so I was really the only one he had. The only one he had to take as family since everyone else at his job would be bringing their families. He nicely showed me his work area and he introduced me to his co-workers and his boss Samantha. Samantha was his boss that he said liked him and wanted to be with him. She could barely talk and she had a trachea tube. He may or may not have been telling the truth or it could have just been his way to make me jealous. Either way, I am not the one he needed to watch. His other male co-worker flirted whenever Vee left me at his cubicle. Of course I didn't tell Vee because things would have gotten switched up and made as if the flirting would have been my fault. Then again, Vee and his co-worker may have planned the test to test me.

>FOR SICKNESS AND IN HEALTH<

Why in the world would Vee decide to eat popcorn with peanuts in it? Something that he is allergic to and eventually caused him to end up in the hospital. I had to pick him up from the hospital, because he was unable to drive. My heart is full of compassion and I tried to be the good wife. Besides my vows did say in sickness and in health. It's funny how God works, because I later found out that when Vee was at his job, he had been meeting with a lady who went to church with us WITHOUT me to discuss our finances.

It was suspect and suspicious. How in the Heaven, hell, or on earth were they doing that? Anyway that's another book for someone else to write.

>VALENTINE'S DAY<

For Valentine's Day Vee bought me a bible and a red heart, filled with chocolate candy from the church's bookstore. He had been advised that a bible was the best gift to give to me, since I didn't have one and obviously (in their eyes) I wasn't reading the word or doing anything that the word of God said. In other's opinion, I was looked at as the cause of and the destruction of the marriage. Vee was normal and I was the crazy one-remember?

>BIBLE TOTING <

Although I could hardly speak to Vee, I carried the Bible that he gave me every time we went to church. That is until the day I made the mistake of truly and accidentally leaving the bible at church after a service. I think I may have left it after we went through a couple of days of the marriage conference. I don't know. Who cares *how* it was left the point is that I left it. Vee somehow got the bible back in his possession and returned it. If I remember correctly, he handed it to me or gave it to an usher or someone to return to me. This is one of the few details-which I really can't remember specifically. *Either way this couldn't be my bible, because now this bible had a beautiful inscription in it. Something like: To my beautiful wife (yadda yadda, yadda)…I love you or love you always… All of this done in the event that someone else saw the bible and would think that Vee was just the most wonderfully romantic husband in the world. Hardly the truth.*

>WHAT A BIRTHDAY - MARCH 15, 2004<

I wasn't living with Vee but I went over there for my birthday and he cooked dinner. Although my mother advised me against eating it I ate his cooking. He defrosted and put in the oven some pork chops (this was before I gave up pork) stuffed with crabmeat and ribs and some type of vegetable something. It was actually pretty good even though he bought it from one of those shop-at-home TV channels, froze it, and then defrosted it for me. Either way it didn't have any poison in it and/or the Holy Ghost intervened. And I lived through it…

Chapter IV

>WHAT'S NEXT - DOGGIE GODS?<

I haven't had much experience with pit bulls although I always heard stories--bad stories about how they attack people. Vee had two pits bulls, when we met. He said that they were show dogs and had been with him since he was in the military stationed in California. Those dogs ate better than we ate. They got boxes of chicken backs from our human meat distributors and specially ordered and prepared dietary foods. They were the King and Queen of the house. Vee drove a breeder in from Virginia to get special dog food, they had a doggie treadmill and each had their own kennels, because he didn't want them to mate. He was rough with the dogs, but I thought that that was part of the "man's best friend" loyalty training. Remember I was ignorant, and I grew up in a house where we mainly had cats for pets. Any dogs that my family had were not allowed to be in the house and in those days didn't get *training* - they just lived as dogs.

After while, I was no longer afraid of them and realized that Vee's dogs actually looked fiercer than they were. In fact, soon I began to let the dogs out of their crates, on my own and without Vee, when I came home, and took them for walks. The dogs began getting used to me and would run and play and jump in my lap (as well as anyone else who sat on the couch). Then they would sniff and lick the faces of whom ever would allow them to. Ironically, it was the cutest and most affectionate thing that I had experienced at that time.

>DO ALL DOGS HAVE TO LIVE THROUGH HELL? <

The boy dog began to sit at my feet at attention especially when Vee was around, almost like he was my bodyguard and ready to protect me. He sat there similar to how the guards do at the Queens' castle gate in London. The dog even began to give Vee a certain distinct look and growl at him, as if to display the fact that he was protecting me. Vee's dogs began showing ME more loyalty than HIM? You should already know that he didn't like that. As punishment, Vee stopped showing the dogs the attention and love that he once had. He would more often than not, leave them locked up in their crates/kennels for days. This means that they would eat, sleep and use the bathroom all in the same area.

As my life got more miserable with Vee, so did the dogs'. The dogs could often be heard *whimpering* and crying as they tried to escape their "*doggie jails*." The wanted and needed to be released from the dungeon in the basement where they had been sentenced. After some time the dogs had no choice but to eat their own feces because Vee did not give them any food or water for days at a time. I didn't have much money, but I would try to feed them whatever I could, like ground beef or chicken. Vee only wanted them to have certain foods, so he would often scold me for feeding them. I would even sneak and let the dogs out before he came home. And I truly believe that they knew who truly loved and cared for them and was on their side. I was becoming depressed for them and when I could - I tried to free them. But after awhile I was no longer at the house to help and advocate for them. Soon the dogs were being starved totally by Vee (I was pretty much gone at this point and the locks had already changed). The dogs were so hungry, filthy, dirty and unhealthy, that you could actually see their ribs. These dogs could turn at any moment and to them I probably looked like chicken and Vee like beef. Not long after I left, I guess the dogs had gotten used to being alone and unloved by Vee, because it was obvious that they had given up hope, and began preparing themselves to die. They just began sitting in their crates and they no longer cried out for help to Vee they just looked at him.

One day I asked Vee how the dogs were and he said that one of them had died after I put my knee high in their food. The kind of knee-highs that are worn by a woman instead of panty hose? I again, wasn't staying at the house nor had I been there without Vee. Vee's story was contradicting. At one time, he said that I broke in the house, stole his bike and killed the dog. Seriously?! First of all, I can't remember the last time that I was actually on a bike. But more importantly, how could someone whom he had called a "*hippo*" (by Vee) ride a bike?

>LIFE INSURANCE<

What really happened was that Vee staged the entire "murder". While he was entertaining the life insurance sales man regarding the purchase of a life insurance policy for me the male dog began to whimper loudly. So loudly that the insurance salesman told him to go and check on the dog. And he did. Vee played the role of an individual concerned with the well being of his distraught dog. Then the salesman told Vee that he should take the dog to the emergency room of a veterinarian office. Vee now had a witnesses to his emotional distress of having to deal with a dying dog, and someone to solidify his story.

>ASHES TO ASHES<

I came back to visit Vee (I don’t know why…you do crazy things when you are in love) during one of our reconciliation attempts and I saw something strange on the entertainment center, (two identical pieces of furniture - one of which he paid for and the other I did and both my idea. He had his sister’ husband put it together. I could have put it together, but he didn’t want to feel less of a man. Anyway he kept them both. I saw something that I would have never thought in a million years that I would see - something that is normally just seen on TV during a crazy scary movie. I had no idea at that time people really did this, or more so, that I was married to someone who did...what you are asking? Keep reading I'm about to tell you.

Vee had the dead dog cremated, placed her ashes in a box and placed a god's statue on top of it. I went *off* in disgust and he eventually moved the "dog's remains" aka ashes in a box, to the back of one of his trucks in the front yard, that never ran. Once Vee did this and I knew that the ashes were in there, I didn't want to walk by that truck any more. For a long time I would walk the long way through the driveway to my car. Mind you although it was a two-car driveway, my car was often parked on the street and Vee's two vehicles were in the driveway. Soon the other dog died and yep you guessed it – he was cremated too. HOW SICK and DEMONIC!

>DUTCHESS<

At the end of April 2004, I tried to come back and reconcile again (please don't ask me why...and yes I finally learned my lesson). Just as others have manipulated the cycle of domestic violence, Vee promised me this time would be different. I moved back into Vee's house on the last day of April around the time that Vee was about to leave to go away to a men's retreat, with the church. While he was gone out of the kindness of my heart I bought him a one-year-old rottweiler named Duchess for $100.00. I must have really been out of my mind. Duchess was beautiful and the most loving dog in the world. I dropped hints to Vee about the dog-being the surprise for his birthday that I had gotten him, and although he was supposed to be gone overnight he drove home. He said that the reason that he had come home was because he missed me but the truth was that he didn't trust me. Me twenty-six years old and home alone? Vee on a side note, did seem different after the retreat. All of the men of the church were to wear a rubber band to remind them of what they had learned while at away at the retreat. The concept was doing well until the day he took it off. It was as if he had taken God completely off of him, and he went back to living life the way that he knew it - contrary to the word of God.

Anyway back to the dogs.

It wasn't good enough that *I* had bought Vee one dog, but he wanted an additional one. We ended up driving all the way to the Eastern shore of Maryland – an hour away-to pick up four year old Lexi from a breeder who was retiring her from being a show dog because of her age and bad hip. Vee wanted Lexi *just because*, even though he wasn't even sure if the two female dogs would get along. Duchess was going to like Lexi and Lexi was going to like Duchess. Those were Vee's demands and he was not going to be questioned. It was just going to be that way. Soon the two dogs got used to each other, and appeared to be happy. Today, I don't know if either or both of the dogs are dead or alive right now, but they too had become Vee's gods as he worshiped them. Despite Vee *ruff housing the* dogs to illustrate his authority over them sometimes, I believe that he intentionally did it to give me a warning of what could happen to me, if I didn't recognize him as *my* master, and my god. I mean my husband, whom I had to submit.

Chapter V

>THE PROPOSAL<

Right after I said I do - he did everything that he wanted to do. Actually Vee called and proposed to me over the phone while I was at work at an amusement park. He called me as he usually did at work, but this time he played music and read poetry It was different and nowhere near what I had expected my wedding proposal would be. But okay I said yes. I had finally gotten what I wanted and felt I deserved. I would often playback the voice mails that he left me so that coworkers could hear how sweet and romantic they were. Awwww…often times I melted from the attention and affection that he showed me. And although he called everyday - several times a day - I never took it to thought that he was starting to harass me by phone. It got worse after he found out that our cell phones had to stay in a locker at work because they were not allowed in the amusement park, while we worked. And it got even worse once he learned the phone number to the office where I worked.

>THE FAKE OUT<

Where's the ring you ask? We got the ring from my younger cousin, who I think got it from a beauty supply store for under $5.00. I didn't care it looked "really" real and as if it had real gold with a huge diamond in the middle.

Aight… we had everyone fooled.

Even though as I wore the ring it was slowly turning colors. To everyone it looked like a huge diamond ring that Vee had brought me. But in actuality, he had not even thought about buying a ring. Who cared I had the man, the house, the car and the freedom… I did eventually get a real bridal wedding ring set.

>ROAD TRIP<

I thought that it was time for me to have a "*real*" wedding ring so Vee and I took a trip to Atlantic City, NJ. While there we walked the boardwalk, and went into one of the pawn shops, until I had found the perfect set with a huge diamond for only a few hundred dollars. I can't remember exactly, but I do believe WE paid for my ring out of the money that I was putting into his bank account. Mysteriously, the diamond on the ring looked a lot smaller, once the guy who worked inside the pawnshop took almost an hour to "*clean*" it. I truly believe that he had switched the diamonds but again it was my word against some guy's.

>MOVING ON UP<

After he proposed I went and got all of my belongings

from my Mother's house with the use of Vee's minivan but not Vee. He said that he had to work or something. I should have stopped the relationship right there but I didn't. I was so anxious to be with this man that I didn't stop to evaluate the situation or what was occurring. Vee loved me. He loved me the way that I had been longing to be loved all my life. And if I had to settle for moving my stuff alone to have that love, it didn't matter. I was an independent woman and I was the one on top - because I had material things to show - that he loved me. With all of the love that I was getting from Vee, I truly started to love him and all that he had to offer. I just wanted to be loved and wanted him to love me back. Not to mention that what was his-was becoming mine too. Weren't they? And I didn't want to look like a fool or a dummy for backing out of the deal. I was getting married and that was the bottom line! That is all anyone had to know. I was getting married! People had said that he was going to be my husband and well now he really was.

>LICENSE TO KILL<

When we decided that we were going to be married, Vee and I together we went to go get the marriage license from the Prince George's County Courthouse. We both swore under oath that we had never been married, were single, and not related. I was honest and innocent of perjury, but the same cannot be said about Vee.

>LICENSED TO WED<

We stood in front of the Prince George's County clerk's officer and after paying $55.00, and filling out the paper work, she printed out a copy and asked us to proof read the information for accuracy.Once we checked to make sure that –our names were spelled correctly, that our ages and addresses were correct and our marital status was well…

Vee had said that he too was never married when in fact he had told me that he had only married another female because she paid him to do so, and they were now divorced. I didn't say anything because it didn't matter to me-he was getting ready to marry me.

>THE JUMP OFF<

Honestly, this was the time that I should have gone and done a credit check, background check, checked the Maryland Judiciary Case Search website (public records file), and other websites. I later did and what I found out about Vee had me in awe.

>LOVING RAPE<

Two weeks before the wedding I was almost by my

fiancé. See, I had this idealistic mentality of my wedding night. Even though I wasn't a virgin, I wanted to save myself and present myself to him despite my past – as being pure and only for him, on our wedding night. But he wanted it then and now. It started by us disagreeing about a situation and I had gone downstairs to sit in the living room on the couch and soon after Vee came downstairs too. I was only wearing a bathrobe. And he wanted me. He wasn't comprehending that I was not feeling him because he had upset me. In his mind was what he wanted and needed from his *coochie* bank. Vee held me down on the loveseat by my neck and acted, as if he was just having *"ruff sex"* but it didn't feel right. He had one hand around my neck and the other hand pulling apart my robe as he climbed on top of me. I managed to push him off, after he loosened his grip – which only happened after hearing me crying, and screaming and begging for him to stop. Funny how the neighbors' whose townhouse was directly connected to our/Vee's house never called the police, despite me banging on the walls and asking them to on several occasions. They have even been outside during some of our episodes – and they sure did pick fine times to mind their business. Maybe they had just become immune to the constant cycle Vee had taken women through?

>FREEDOM<

From that moment, I really didn't want to have sex anymore with Vee. I really did want to leave him, but I couldn't because I had too much pride. What would everybody say if I moved back home to my mother's house? Truth be told, she and I weren't getting along like we should have been and I had finally found a way out. I refused to go back! There is NO WAY that I could even go back to her [my mom's] house, so I had to deal with Vee and the beginning of his issues being revealed. I've heard several people say that love has you blind. And, I was blind and with sunglasses on to conceal the real situation. At this point, I felt I had to marry him.

>WEDDING DAY<

Thursday, August 14, 2003 was going to be the date, for a small intimate wedding with Vee, myself and the officiating minister. That way we could have the real wedding with family and friends next year when our wedding date fell on a Saturday. That would be the dream wedding with a white wedding gown, with a veil, bouquets of flowers all around, cake cutting, walking down the church aisle, people laughing, crying and partying at the reception; me smiling and laughing, my girls in the wedding party etc. Not to mention the perfect music and eventually my perfect day. My mother and I had already gone to start looking at dresses...her coworker was going to coordinate it... it was all planned out.

>TOM THUMB WEDDING<

Whoa…my bad…I was fantasizing for a second, as all little girl's do. This wedding would just be the wedding that we do to get all of the benefits of being married. Tax breaks, joint bank accounts and we can even have sex "legally" and no longer be in sin for shacking up and fornicating. It is the perfect arrangement.

LaDonna you have done well. You married yourself a baller or at least it appeared that way.

(Footnote: the definition of a Tom Thumb Wedding is: a theatrical portrayal of an actual wedding and this was about to be the second that I was involved with. My first one was at five years old and now another at twenty five.)

>RISE AND SHINE<

There is no way I could stop now, I had to marry Vee. It was one of the hottest days of the summer, and the heat was definitely scorching. Did I miss another warning sign from God about the life of hell that I was about to endure because of a bad choice? Or was it an indication of the consequences of my sin. When I woke up on the morning of the wedding I sat in the tub and began to have second thoughts. I truly believe that it was the voice of God – WARNING ME and intervening. But I ignored it. This was one of the few times where Vee allowed me to actually *get clean* without him interrupting and often he would cut the shower off while I was in it. He would open the door while it was cold as a way of forcing me to talk to him. There I stood shivering and cold until he got his way. This happened no matter what season and temperature it was outside.

My mom, her coworker, one of my best friends - an ordained reverend, and my little cousin, were the witnesses to the ceremony. My mom's co-worker videotaped it and ok well I had to do it to *save face*. As they arrived, I got out the tub and began to get dressed in the white dress that I had bought for Easter like four to five years prior-well actually an ex boyfriend bought it for me, after I had an abortion.

>WEDDING DRESS<

My dress was a white, lacey, crochet looking dress with a matching shawl to wear around my neck. My mother had bought me a tiara, stockings and a *good* girdle to wear under the dress. Vee put on a pair of black tuxedo pants, a tuxedo shirt and purple and gold cummerbund. The night before, I had wet set my hair to make it curly. Vee went to the barber shop and got a haircut. We looked better than good. So maybe I was just having bad nerves about what was going to take place. I have heard stories before about people being nervous when they got married. But my cousin had just walked down the aisle when she got married that last August boldly, and without crying, so I was confident that I could do it too.

Marriage was nothing to play with.

>HERE COMES THE BRIDE<

Vee and I had planned that my bridal procession song would be *"My Wife"* by a guy he said he knew from the barbershop who had put out a CD, named Mark *Somebody*. According to Vee, the guy was going to charge $500 for him to sing the song live at our wedding, so we opted just to play the CD. Ironically and after all of the times that we had listened to the CD, it was now missing, when I needed and wanted it most. Somehow Vee couldn't find the CD as it had vanished. Vee put on an instrumental song from his laptop so that I could come down the stairs to become his wife. The ceremony was short, sweet and to the point...

"Do you..."

"...I do"

As I responded to Vee with my vows, I got a little overwhelmed and almost cried as I looked in his eyes. We began to kiss each other before given permission by the minister as he was saying the final parts of the traditional wedding ceremony from his book. It was as if the stress and tension of getting married had been lifted and a feeling of relief had fallen upon me. I had no idea that my entire destiny was about to be changed. After about twenty minutes, we were officially married. My mother had bought us a cake and after the ceremony we cut it, participated in a toast, but we were eager for everyone to leave so that we could have sex…or because we were married was it now making love? Either way we ready to *get it on.* Instead of us consummating our marriage, Vee, my mom and I went out to dinner, to a restaurant that would later be the scene to drama. At dinner, we flirted with one another by putting up the restaurant's menu in front of us, kissed and talked trash about what we were going to do to one another when we got back home. We ate, entertained my Mom and returned home to consummate the marriage.

>STARTING LINE<

The first couple of weeks of marriage were *ok* for the most part. I had still been working as a temp and sometimes the agency didn't have any work. At the amusement park, I had already been taken off the schedule k because of the excessive phone calls, and attendance, and although the pay was only seven dollars an hour, every penny added up and helped. I tried to be a house wife but Vee was not hearing that. He immediately wanted me to change all of my identification to reflect me being married to him. This included my license and social security card. I really thought he was proud that he had married me, but this was all the beginning stages of Vee's controlling ways. The signs had always been there, I just ignored them.

Chapter VI

I called the car loan lender and told them where to come get the car out of the driveway, because I was tired of hiding it and looking over my shoulder. Hopefully, they would come and get it while I was asleep so that I wouldn't have to watch my car being taken from me and just have the situation over and done. Vee was excited and overly helpful since this meant that would be totally stripped of everything that I had obtained before and without him. At this point, I would have to be D-E-P-E-N-D-E-N-T on him. They came during the night and I no longer owned my *Focus.* Driving Vee's car was a special privilege that I got if I made sure that he "got some" and was in control. When he didn't get his way I lost my *special privileges* and couldn't drive his vehicle. You see the big green truck was something that I couldn't touch when I was on *punishment*. Instead I was permitted to drive the minivan, which barely ran, would cut off, and smelled musty. The steering wheel was hardly attached to the vehicle and it had a radio, which worked when *it* wanted to. It was the worst of the vehicles; second only to the truck that didn't run.

>CONSPIRACY THEORY<

One day I went online to a popular website and found a car being sold in Virginia, by a guy who said that it needed new engine valves. The guy and I made plans to meet after work. You already know Vee was going with me so that he could portray the image of a wonderfully concerned husband. Come on now. Forget the fact that I was trying to buy a car. Vee only saw the worse out of the situation. I was going somewhere to meet another man and Vee definitely was not having that one. And meeting the man in Virginia, which was out of site but definitely not out of his mind! Vee and I finally arrived to meet the guy after battling traffic for an hour. Once we arrived, the guy seemed very eager to sell the vehicle to me. In fact - almost overly eager. He started the car and it sounded good. There is no way this car needed engine valves, because it ran tooooo good. I test drove the car to the nearest ATM and then to a gas station. A mechanic took a peek at the car *blessed-ly* --at no charge. The mechanic told me that the car didn't need new engine valves just a tune up and an oil change. I was ecstatic. I had my mind made up and I was definitely buying this car. Vee and I returned back to the guy who was selling the car with the big secret. He was selling the car originally for $500 but Vee talked him down to letting us give him two hundred and eighty dollars, since that was the maximum I could get out of the ATM.

The guy also agreed to let us drive home on the tags registered in his name in Virginia, with the understanding that we would mail them back to him, once we got the car back to Maryland. Vee didn't think that we should mail the tags back, until I got the car on the road with my tags and new brakes. And he did everything he could do to make sure the tags didn't get mailed back.

Some time had passed and I felt extremely bad and dishonest. My mother ended up mailing the tags back to the guy in Virginia for me and you already know that the guy was a couple of stages beyond pissed. Vee didn't care about him, his DMV record...or me. Ironically and only by the grace of God, I was allowed to get temp tags on the car. Something that I didn't think that was possible since I hadn't had insurance on my previous car and got hit with a lot of insurance violations and fees. Once the car was mobile Vee seemed to want to drive my car more than I did. Was it really because the gas was cheaper or was it a matter of control? He would often drive my car to the point that I had little or no gas in it. Then he would make sure that I did not have any money to refill the gas tank.

>WRECKED<

The car was mobile and mine for only a little over a month and a week. The reason that I can be so sure is because the thirty-day temp tags had run out. I was so broke that I decided to start selling pizzas and cookie dough to try to get money and fundraise the same way that schools do, for my personal finances. One day, although at that point, I was not really staying with Vee. I made arrangements to meet the delivery guy at the house in order to pick up my fulfilled order. However, on my way to the house my life would take even more of a turn for the worse. As I remember, I was about to stop at a six-lane stoplight, and I was in the lane to keep straight, on my side of the road. Somehow my car hit the car in front of me-and that one hit one and that one in front of it, and so on, and so on…for five cars. A police officer came over to the scene, but did not assign fault even though my tags were as dead as a doornail. Everyone blamed me for the accident and I quickly conjured up a story in mind. A car was coming over into my lane and I had nowhere to go. A young boy who was two cars up from me informed the police that he had seen the car also, so the story that I remember, must have had some truth to it. The car that I hit directly was the young boy who validated my story and he hit a car with two women in it and they hit an older lady and she hit another car. This was going to be drastic. Luckily, the driver of car who the older lady hit- told us not to worry about him because he was *dirty*. This meant that he had no license and no insurance and so he pulled off like it never happened. The front of my car although mobile, had a smashed hood and headlights since it went under the car of the person who I hit. *WOW*! I was sore and thankful to God that no one was seriously hurt although one of the women in the passenger seat said that her neck and her back hurt, even though she declined to go to the hospital in an ambulance. She told that police that she would go to the hospital later. *I'm the one who still has the seat belt bruise under my breast, an ankle that hurts when it wants to, and a back that I have to crack every night in order to get comfortable enough to go to sleep.* FYI: Unless you are seriously hurt in an accident, your back, neck and various other muscles will not hurt instantly. Despite the accident, I proceeded to hurry up and drive to Vee's house the place I was supposed to be allowed to call home.

The accident had me more shook up than I had realized.

When I put my key in the lock it appeared that Vee had changed the locks to the doors on the house. Later I realized that I had made a mistake and entered the wrong key into the door's locks. Funny how so many keys look the same. The delivery guy came and I transferred the order to my car and paid him the balance due. There wasn't really any point to go back to work at this point since I had already stayed gone over my allotted hour for lunch. I called my job and informed that I would not be returning back to work that day. I proceeded to my mother's house to put the pizzas and cookie dough in her fridge. Most of the orders were going to her job anyway – and once I got there, I called her and explained to her what happened. She advised me to go to the hospital. Then I called Vee and he "rushed" right over to escort me to the hospital, since he now had a reason to leave work early. Ironically my mother and he arrived at her apartment at the same time. And that time I couldn't understand why my mother got mad at me because I chose to ride with my *husband* while he followed us. She is the one who refused to ride *with* us. Besides Vee was my *oh so loving husband* and doing the right thing of consoling, supporting and taking care of his wife. I was still in denial and yet still holding on to a hope that he was going to change by taking care of and loving me and ultimately being a good husband. When we arrived at the hospital, Vee immediately jumped on the phone with the insurance company and my troubles worsened. He made up a complete story and gave it to them in an attempt to *jam* me up even more. I think I was more afraid of what was about to happen legally than the bruise on my chest, the back pain and the sprained ankle. Only a small amount of time went by before calls from the other victims and their insurance companies, started coming in to me, even at work. However, all of the calls stopped and the situation just disappeared...was it because I was on Vee's insurance policy and he ultimately found out that he too be would be liable if I was found *at fault*?

The bottom line is that the entire accident appears to have never happened.

Chapter VII

Vee made sure that my interaction with the world outside of Vee was minimal. Although he had various ways of doing it, his most drastic was by getting rid of every phone in the house.The phone line was still activated at the house, but Vee hid all of the phones and forwarded the line to his cell phone, so that he would have the only means of contact and be able to screen all of the calls. There were times when I tried to call and get help from family and friends, only to have my calls interrupted by Vee. At those points, I could do nothing but cry. There were several times, when I cried so hard that I began to vomit hard until blood vessels burst in my eyes.

>FAMILY TIES<

Vee didn't get along with his family and/or their friends very well. When I was around he and his mother and sister had several arguments, which was another clear sign that I should have walked away. There is an old cliché which says something like: as a man treats his mother and the women he is biologically related to is a clear indication of how he is going to treat the female who is his mate.

>BOYZ IN THE HOOD AT THE PARTY<

There was a time when Vee's niece had a birthday party and Vee's sister was pregnant. At the birthday party somehow Vee's sister got upset with the niece's father who was not her husband just her *baby's daddy* and Vee confronted him. Next thing I know Vee was taking off his watch and the two guys were heading to the front of the yard to fight. No one - especially his niece's white friend who obviously wasn't used to urban surroundings - knew what to expect. I watched the little girl and her father make a mad dash to their car to leave. Bad enough the party was in Capitol Heights, Maryland and was predominately, if not all African American, except for that one little girl. Vee's mom and I broke the fight up and I had to literally place my knee between Vee's legs near his crotch as he sat on the couch, to restrain him. Deep down I knew he didn't want to fight that guy, otherwise he would not have allowed me to restrain him or whisper in his ear about him “getting some” when we got home if he chilled out. This made Vee smile and forget about the fight. His mother, sister, I and several others talked to him and tried to explain that this was neither the time nor the place and the situation eventually defused. His niece's father had already left the party. Vee's sister thanked him for taking up for her and having good intentions for her, and after we helped clean up the mess created by the party, Vee and I left as well.

>CD ROM HEIST<

There was another time when we drove out to Vee's father and stepmother’s house where his baby brother also lived. While there Vee stole some CD’s from his stepmother and she knew he had taken them and I confirmed her intuition when she called. Vee tried to shift the blame to his brother, saying that he gave him permission to take them. There are many more stories of Vee and his family’s drama. But I’ll leave that for one of them to put into a book. Having friends was never an issue to me and recently I had hooked up one of my best male friends together in a relationship, which was really getting serious and committed. Truth be told I was a little jealous of their relationship, once I did it especially since I could have been in the relationship with him and probably happily married now with children. I had my chance my freshman year of college but I was bourgeois aka boo-jee and thought that my best male friend was not my type. Despite him having a car and more while I didn't... he was such a sweetheart. In an effort to do a good deed since I had blown it, I tried to *hook him up* to make things right. He has a good heart, job and other materialistic things and she well… wanted what she wanted. So they were the perfect couple. We still talk and he knows that I will always love him. She knows that I will always love her and my niece too.

>BROKEN CONNECTION<

My friends and I had certain routines whenever one of us went out on a date, especially when we went with someone new. We would call each other to check on each other, and to make sure the other was safe. Genuinely we cared about each other. Vee and I were still in our dating and courting stage of our relationship when we were about to have sex or what I thought at that time was making love. Just as we had gotten into the motion of things, my cell phone rang. If I had been thinking clearly, I would have called it quits on the relationship that night.Vee didn't like the fact that my phone rang and grabbed it out of my hand as I checked to see who was calling. The next thing I know my phone was hurled onto the floor of the bathroom, which was adjacent to the bed, causing the screen to break and be unusable. All of this because he looked at the caller ID and saw that it was my best male friend calling to check on me. I was devastated and in pure disbelief, but he promised me that he would buy me another phone. You already know it never happened right? From that day on my friends, especially the male ones slowly but surely, stopped calling.

>OVER THE BOTTOM<

On another occasion, after we were married, one of my friends and former co-worker Diamond, whom I had known for years, stopped by on her way out on a date. Even though she had a man at home, she wanted to *dibble and dabble* with a guy who used to work with us. They used to flirt at work, and until that night, she had fought the temptation, because she was *happy* at home. I made the mistake again of sharing with my *husband* the situation and why she was stopping by. My bad…I was dumb. To be genuinely honest and to have no secrets was my rationale for telling him. Anyway Diamond came to see me and she and I couldn't have a moment alone to talk. Vee sat right underneath us, as if he was one of the girls. This embarrassed me terribly. He made comments and remarks - which not only made me feel low but ashamed. In fact I believe that to this day, despite us communicating very rarely via email, that that was my last time seeing her in person. Here's why...

The straw which broke the camel's back was when my friend Diamond went to use the bathroom. Vee made a comment that embarrassed her and me by saying "*Damn…Diamond*" then he looked at me and finished: "*her ass is fat*". Diamond looked at me and we both decided it was time for her to leave.

>LOST<

Vee and I decided to take a trip to Virginia Beach to visit his uncle and his uncle's family. On the way down there it was like World War I, II, III, IV and V! I can't remember what exactly we were arguing over, but it ended up with me wanting to get out of the truck in the middle of nowhere. Vee took my wallet and threw it in the back of his junky trunk with all of my IDs and bankcards etc. in an effort to leave me stranded. The Bible says "*naked in this world. I came and naked I shall leave.* "It didn't say "*Vee you take all of her stuff because you are her husband and if she leaves you she leaves with nothing.*

>911<

I began to walk to try and find a police station. People looked at me like I was crazy and kept pointing down the street. They were of no help in direction and so I kept walking until I was far enough from him and near to a pay phone. My mother had just put a block on her home phone so I couldn't call her collect. But one of my former good friends and I had a system whereas I could call her collect and she I and we would pay each other back. She and I never did collect on any debts to one another. We just charged them to our friendships. I called everyone that I could think of, but no one answered their phone. Then I started making phone calls with the charges reversed to Vee and I's home phone, and one of the first people that I thought to call my best male friend since he knew Richmond and could probably help me out. Somehow, Vee called the phone company and put a block on our home phone for the reversed charges. Then he tapped into the pay phone line, which I was on and talked to me until he finally convinced me to get back into his vehicle and proceed to his family's home. The question still is how did he manage to be on the phone? My only explanation is that the facts that he used to work for a cable company and was probably trained on how to reconfigure certain wired connections, like phone, cable and internet. But who knows. The only other option that I had was to get back in his truck but things still weren't better and I still hated him. When we pulled up his family came outside to greet us and witnessed him trying to snatch my car key from me. His uncle explained to Vee that he wasn't going to tolerate Vee putting his hands on me. So Vee pretty much chilled for the rest of the visit with his family. A break and rest that I needed.

>TINTED<

On the way back home, I had to drive. It seemed like I had to whenever we went out together. As I was driving, I was doing about 90 miles per hour plus when all of a sudden I saw police lights. I immediately and nervously pulled over. Because I have never had a moving violation, I didn't know what to expect. Vee's truck that I was driving had tinted windows and I didn't see the other car that had pulled behind us.The police officer walked over to Vee's side of the truck and asked why we had stopped. I told him that I thought he was pulling me over and he asked me in return did I have a reason to be pulled over. I smiled, said no and proceeded, to drive back home…back to Vee's house.

Chapter VIII

>GETTING’BUSY<

I had been raised in church, so I already knew that once you join a church you are supposed to join ministries so that you will stay active at the church and feel a part of it. Personally the more active I stay in church, the more accountable I feel to and convicted by God. Become attached and stay encouraged.

Vee was not having that. Every ministry that I tried to join at church - except the all women group, Vee found out who was overseeing it and stopped my membership immediately. I was quickly becoming a *pew member*.

>SABATAGE<

I tried to join the media ministry and was allowed to attend one meeting. Then Vee talked to the president and all of a sudden phone calls and emails ceased from him and to this day he can barely speak to me. Next I tried to join the musical staff, but Vee went to the minister of music – someone who had gone to the same high school as I did and played in the same bands at school-and told him that I was a whore and trying to sleep with him. He quickly became distant and shut down from talking to me, hugging me and interacting with me.

First of all let me clear the record. I like tall, dark skinned men. My rule is that you have to be my complexion or darker. Definitely never lighter. The minister of music was light skinned with good wavy hair and more importantly married with a bunch of kids… light skinned men went out of style with Al B. Sure and Tony Terry a long time ago. At least in my opinion. Vee went to everyone that he thought he could use, including the Elders of the church to discredit me and told them all types of stories. I am sure that I did not hear all of them then nor do I want to hear about or know. But I could tell because people in church looked at me differently. Everyone became distant and treated me like a stray dog with fleas.

>FALL BACK<

I stopped attending the church regularly and I missed so many new members' classes because Vee left me at home or took the keys to all of the vehicles, so that I couldn't get there. I felt truly like the woman in the bible who had the issue of blood and had to press her way through the crowd to get to Jesus. Many years later a Pastor Duane Simmons (Simmons Memorial Baptist Church) told me that blood is symbolic of life. During the marriage I was truly having *some issues* in my *life*. People at the church didn't want to hug or touch me anymore and truth be told they didn't even want to speak. All of this-at a time when I needed affection, and for someone to show me, that they loved me. Several times they would turn their heads when they saw me walking in their direction.

I remember a time Vee called an Elder in the midst of one of our *situations* that resulted in me getting out of

Vee's truck and the Elder told me to get back in the car with Vee. If I remember correctly, we had just left the church-- no we were on our way to church-- and were doing more arguing, when Vee pulled over to a popular convenience store's parking lot. Because of the situation I decided that I was no longer in the mood to go to church and I wanted Vee to take me home. The Elder kinda *fussed me out* and reminded me that I wasn't supposed to live under a spirit of offense. *I was being abused by my husband so how else was I supposed to live?* There was no other way to live but under a constant state of offense and take defensive measures.

>SUNDAY DINNER<

We had just come from church and were about to go out to eat. But as soon as we had passed by our house to go to a restaurant - the daily beefing started.

I really didn't feel like having my spirit disturbed after being in church, so I asked to be dropped off over my mother's house. Vee actually pulled over to the side of the road where other cars were starting to merge on from the highway near George Palmer Highway aka Martin Luther King Highway and the beltway exit right at the exit where other cars were coming onto George Palmer Highway. Vee wanted me to get hit by a moving vehicle and killed, so he tried to push me out of the vehicle. Not near a curb but near the white merging line right after a sidewalk or median…I'm for real.

We went back and forth in a tug of war match over my pocket book. I could get out but Vee was not going to let me, my purse, IDs, keys **and** ATM cards get out of that vehicle. This way after he put the vehicle in motion, I would be left on the side of the road to fend for myself and protect my life from the traffic. Or maybe he would be happy to hear me beg for my life. Maybe he hoped that I would die on that day so that my death wouldn't look like it was his fault. I wasn't going to be allowed to get out. Next thing I know Vee had put the truck back in motion and we had hit the back of another smaller truck stopped at a stop light about to make a left turn. As Vee got out checking the damage and making sure that the other driver was not hurt, I slipped my ATM cards and driver's license onto my hip between my panties and my stockings. If he wanted it, he was going to have to kill me to get it this time. The other vehicle had no insurance, so we left the scene with no police report and only damage to the front of Vee's truck, which he got fixed ASAP. Where did that money come from? Although, I ended up with a hurt knee we still proceeded to the restaurant. That was Vee's way to apologize without apologizing. As we sat in the parking lot of the restaurant, Vee began to appear to be remorseful and apologize. But I didn't want to hear it. I left him and went into the restaurant alone. How I had an appetite after all that had happened, I don't know, but I did. He eventually came in and sat down with me at the table. Then he accused me of flirting with the waiter, when he came to take our order. Vee ordered a salad with no tomatoes but when it came – the tomatoes were on the salad. He flicked the tomatoes onto the table. Then he acted as if he was praying but he really looked like he was high and nodding off at the table. I kept saying "*Vee can you please stop. Why are you looking like that? You are embarrassing me.*" But he didn't. I hesitantly ate, he paid the bill and we eventually left. Vee and I never ate at that restaurant again...Strange since this was the restaurant that we went to after we had gotten married.

Chapter IX

>MY M.O.<

To end my ties with Vee, I filed for my divorce in June of 2007, and because I had met a guy I really liked. He was a deacon at the church I joined and began attending in Baltimore, and very much my type. He was tall, had a dark complexion and his hair in dreds. He also had sex appeal, a car, two jobs, no kids, and most of all he had God. Later I found out that he had a form of Godliness but no power. So to make sure that I didn't lose the new guy, I had to get rid of the old one. At least he was trying to grow in God and encouraged me to do so as well.

>CONFIRMATION<

In February I was about to move out of my second home in Baltimore. As I sat home bored, for some reason I dialed 411 and Vee's number was still listed. The operator said there was two numbers listed and read them off to me. As he read off the numbers, I wrote them down and avoided being charged for using directory assistance.

>EVIDENCE<

When I called Vee’s house a female answered the phone.

“*Hello, May I speak to Vee, please*” I asked.

“*He’s not in did you want to leave a message*?” she replied.

My adrenalines kicked in and to further investigate who this girl was, and of course to be smart I said, “*Yes, can you please tell him that his wife called*”.

This set the girl off, just as I figured that it would. I didn’t care I was trying to build up evidence against Vee for an easy, contested, inexpensive divorce.

She started saying things like *“his wife? You are not married anymore.”*

I said, *“I am married to him and I have papers on him.”*

She began to cuss and fuss and told me not to call her house anymore. If I remember, she called me a Bitch. Truth be told, I purposely fueled it and agitated her so she would keep talking and give me info. And she gave me just enough. I then called Vee on his cell phone-a phone number, which hadn't changed in years. On his voice mail, I left the details of the phone call that I just had with the girl – his girl on *his*, I mean *their* home phone.

>THE ALLIBI<

Within minutes my phone rang and it was Vee with his specially planned story together. He said that he didn't know why she said what she did or why the conversation went the way it did, and that she was just his roommate. He then went on to say that he was forced to rent out rooms to make ends meet because I had left his house and left him with bills. Here's the clincher, if I came home then he wouldn't have to rent rooms out any longer. He still wanted me to move back home with him. Ahhh…too funny…he still wanted me to come home. First of all, it was never "*a*" or my home and I had finally escaped-why would I go back? Really...I know I did some stupid things throughout this marriage, but I wasn't stupid-anymore.

>DUH<

Little did Vee know that I had already gotten the truth from my cousin's husband; that was why I wanted to call for myself in the first place, so why was I was still in disbelief? Maybe I was still holding on to Vee, the relationship, the things that he was doing saying; and mostly, I didn't want to face the situation that was unfolding before my very eyes. But, I was ready now… people kept telling me before that I should leave Vee for good. I kept running from facing the pain and gaining closure, while attempting to make right my mistake of getting married to him. What was I doing, because I felt lost?

>OLDIE NOT GOODIE<

The girl was older than Vee and had moved in his house with her kids. My cousin's husband told me that she had at least two kids and one was old enough to attend high school. She was old and bold-what a combination. Vee was doing him and I couldn't get mad because I had already started dating and doing me. The ultimate revenge was to say *forget the entire marital situation* and date whomever and let whoever move in with me. I didn't want to be alone, and he had already moved on so why shouldn't I? This sounded really good at the time but ultimately; I was hurt more than helped by my tactics. Vee believed that my family whether blood or in-laws would be more loyal to him than me. There wasn't one person in my family who was really feeling him or the way that he treated me. They just tolerated him on the strength of my love for him, and because I had made the choice of being in a relationship with him. In my family if one person loves you we all love you. And if the person doesn't love you…well…Then again maybe Vee knew exactly what he was doing by telling my cousin's husband because Vee really wanted me to find out, and he knew that the information would eventually get to me because of the closeness of my family's ties. The conversation was going back and forth as I dissected his lies. And he tried to explain but I didn't reveal to him how I knew the truth-just that I did know the truth. It continued for a while-until he heard my friend's cell phone chirp. Because of the ambiance noise occurring at my house, Vee said something smart and then hung up on me. Wow, he gotten caught, tried to flip the situation to make everything my fault, and got mad at me…how typical…how orthodox.

>DIVORCE COURT MINUS DIVORCE COURT. <

Why in the world did he file for an annulment after being served with my divorce papers? I had been dating the new guy for about a month or so I really started to like him. So to reassure the new guy of how I felt about him, I sacrificed and paid the $130.00 filing fee. I left work early and went straight to the courthouse. When I got to the counter, the office clerk gave me a packet to complete and there were a lot of women and kids in this area. Happily and pleasantly surprised, the packet was a lot thinner than I had gotten previously online. And a lot simpler too! *That's what's up*...let's get this over with.

>JUST LET ME OUT<

Once I completed the packet, I asked to meet with one of the customer service reps about seeing if I could get my fees waived since I was only working as a temp employee. But I was denied. The only thing that I asked for in the paperwork from Vee and this marriage was my name to be returned back to my maiden's name- Smith. In fact, to encourage Vee to hurry up and just sign the paperwork, I printed nicely – I just want out. The pro se office clerks laughed and teased me because they had said that they have heard people say those words, but had never seen anyone write it on the paperwork. But at this point, that was all I wanted…

>FILING FEES<

I proceeded over to another clerk's office and wrote the two checks: one for the filing fee to the court and the other to the sheriff's office to have Vee served. That way there couldn't be any mess with him saying that he wasn't served. There wasn't any way that Vee could say that he did not receive the paperwork from the court.

Boy was I wrong…

>A BUCK THIRTY<

Here I am about to spend a hundred and thirty dollars that I really didn't have to spend. I still had rent and other bills and I had just bought a car. But it was well worth the sacrifice. Once I walked out of the courthouse in Baltimore City, I felt that a burden had been removed from me. As soon as I got out of the building I called my mother and told her what I had done. She was happy. I was happy.

>REFRESHED<

After I left the city courthouse, I wanted the world to know what I had just done, especially for my special friend. When we first started dating I didn't tell him up front that I was married because I thought it would ruin my chances at a relationship with him. I didn't see a need to tell him or anyone else who didn't already know-especially since I was trying to get out of the "marriage". I didn't want people getting used to calling me Reeder when I had planned on my name changing to Smith in the near future. There was enough confusion in the world and with this situation already. Even though my friend had already somewhat figured out that I was married-but didn't know for sure that I was still legally married and that no paperwork had been filed. I could now be with him with a clean conscious and the umbrella of adultery would be lifted.

>CHECK UP<

I called every week to check the status of Vee being served and figured that since it was going from one city to another county, which the process could take some time. After some time, the Prince George's County Sheriff's office advised me that they had up to thirty days to have Vee served.

So I waited.

Finally, after calling for three weeks straight I got the word that he had in fact been served –June 24, 2007. However, I never received a copy of the affidavit or return of service – whether I was supposed to or not and nor did the Baltimore City Court family system, where I had filed the paperwork.

I conversed with the Prince George's County clerk who handled the paperwork and she shared that she went through a similar marital situation with her ex husband and the way that she got out was because he had died. Now she was happily married. She doesn't know how much she inspired me to open my mind and heart to consider being married again. To be honest there were many times that I had hoped Vee would die for all that he had done to me.

There was even a time when he sat on the floor twisting a shotgun in the middle of the floor spinning it around. I'm still not sure if he was contemplating suicide or planning to kill me, or just being a "*drama king*". Either way, it was a scary thought. I could only remember visualizing how I would react to coming into the room and seeing his body on the floor. Although I saw his death as me finally getting free from him, I couldn't and wouldn't have anything to do with the cause or being the cause of him dying. Previously I had try to get the court to give him an emergency mental evaluation but was denied. The judge said that it would disrupt his life…but what about my life? Anyway, I asked nicely and the Prince George's County Sheriff's office not only faxed me a copy of the paperwork but they also mailed me a copy.

>NO CALL, NO SHOW<

I immediately filed for an order of default to the Baltimore City Court house because Vee had not responded. Soon after, I received a letter from his lawyer.

Ok so Vee had gotten a lawyer - but why? All he had to do was sign the paperwork and show up in court. The documents from the court didn't ask for any alimony, or property, or anything else.

Why couldn't he just let go of *me*, *us*, and this entire *bad nightmare*?

>CC'd<

Little did I know that I was about to get cc'd on a lot of correspondence from Vee's lawyer to the Baltimore City courthouse. There was no problem getting this correspondence to me, but when it came time to get the info to me regarding his annulment case in the Prince George's County court system, I never received anything… Come to find out all of the motions and correspondence were to act as a distraction and to buy Vee and his lawyer some time to push his case, through the Prince George's County court system, undetected. Vee and his lawyer probably knew that the Baltimore City and the Prince George's County court systems did not communicate or share info and they *banked on it.*

Because of my experience with the lack of communication between the different court systems, I have begun trying to raise awareness, so that someone will pass a bill whereas there is a national database to verify information collected during marriage application information. The database would also *house* information on any and all past marriages, divorces etc. I think that this would avoid anyone else's case proceeding how my case proceeded. The two courts didn't even have a conversation about my case.

>THE GAME BEGINS<

As I began to read through the paperwork and respond to each of the motions, I started having to do more research. Especially on the Maryland laws that Vee and his lawyer kept mentioning in their paperwork. First, they said that Vee was not served properly because the sheriff's office left the paperwork with the woman at his house, who said that she was his roommate. Later, he would respond in his paperwork that the person's name on the Affidavit of Service was not who the sheriff recorded in the paper work. According to Vee and his lawyer she was just a female who was staying at his house for two nights while in route to her own house. In other words, she wasn't his roommate but a *houseguest.* Either way, wouldn't that kind of validate my adultery argument of Vee having the opportunity to sleep with another woman?Anyway, next he and his lawyer said that they had a case in Prince George's County pending against me. The paperwork had so many lies in it that I still can't figure out why no one has figured it out or put the pieces together yet? I believe it is because the devil has armies and soldiers all over the place.

If he is allowed to use you as one of his soldiers, then he will do just that.

No one seemed to care.

Think about a lawyer's job-it is to lie if they have to and to do whatever they can to get their client cleared.

Vee's job is to hurt people like he was hurt-mentally and emotionally from a young age.

Now that I think about it, the hurt and pain of his life was very similar to a prominent and influential performer who recently passed away, whereas Vee too just wanted to be loved, but didn't know how to ask for it other than by *acting out*. Vee's hurt was partially because he had a birth defect, and because he felt like his parent's loved his sister and younger brother much more than he.

This made him angry with the world.
His stepmother talked to me after we were married and told me that she tried to warn me not to marry him because he was SICK. But it was already too late because we were married. She said that because I didn't

listen to her warnings, I would now have to deal with Vee's mess.

>CONCLUDED<

December 5th, 2007 - the date before my divorce proceedings had finally arrived. The weatherman had predicted snow, but I don't care if I had to walk to the courthouse that night and stay the night.

I was not missing that day.

While I was at work, I checked my voice mail messages, and there was one in particular, which seemed urgent.The message was from the Baltimore City judge's chambers asking me to call them right away. I immediately called back, and left messages from the time I had gotten home from work until the next morning to find out what was going on.

"*You don't have to come to court your divorce is already done*" are the words I heard.

But how could this have happened?

I hadn't even been to court yet.

>SEE WHAT HAS HAPPENED WAS<

My marriage had already been annulled because Vee filed for an annulment in Prince George's County a month after I filed for my divorce in Baltimore City. Again - evidence that the two court systems never talked to each which allowed him to once again get over. Vee filed the paperwork and said that he had me served on a Sunday afternoon at 12:50 pm. Now those who know me know that I hadn't missed a Sunday in 9 consecutive months and the church wasn't but so big. In fact when you opened the front door of the sanctuary you were standing in the sanctuary, because services were held in a row home that was converted into a church.

On the day that he said that he had me served with the paperwork from the court - I saw him. I saw his truck in Baltimore but it didn't dawn on me that it was in fact him – I just thought that my mind was playing tricks on me. I asked the court systems to keep my address private but instead he was able to not only find me and my residence but anything else he needed in order to win the game and have the upper hand.

>SANCTUARY<

So the question is - if I was served with paperwork an entire church of about 15 people would have seen what happened. It never happened. Vee and his lawyer had said that they had me served, filed an order of default and had gone to court without me knowing any of it. Here it is that I had just gotten out of the hospital after two and a half days of having three EKGs, a CAT Scan, blood work every two hours, medication, and being on a treadmill until my heartbeat got up to one hundred and sixty beats per minute (bpm) – and now this. My heartbeat was supposed to be between fifty to sixty bpm but was extremely low. It had fallen a couple of times and the code blue alarms had sounded. I remember the doctors evaluating me to see if I was really about to die. The hospital visit happened and right after I went to a retreat that changed my life. Don't know how I ended up on the floor after consoling someone else and all the elders and pastors were laying hands on me, making me drink oil and ultimately vomiting. I just kept repeating God I am tired. Take it away. Funny because I thought that I was the ok one.

>HOW<

How did the case happen so fast?

Without concern for cost, I went down to the Prince George's County court house demanding that I get a copy of every piece of paper in the folder. Glory to God…the lady gave them to me free of charge because she saw that something was not right but was not in a predicament to address it. She even said that lawyers do it all the time – say they served someone when they really didn't. Then she told me that she was going to hand walk the letter I had written to the court earlier that week. To this day, no one has still investigated the fact that Vee is (**NOT WAS**) a bigamist, because everyone involved in the case kept concentrating on me not responding in the proper way or on the proper forms. Priorities…remember the devil has soldiers in place all over. I didn't waste time or money trying to get an investigation and I just put the entire situation in God's hands. God's wrath takes less time than my energy and is much worse than any legal system. A few weeks later I applied for my name to be changed back to my maiden name and the courts sent my application back because I didn't have the one hundred and five dollar fee to apply. I had already paid one hundred and thirty dollars once that they did not need to process according to the date of my annulment – why did I have to pay for it again?

> MY NAME IS LADONNA M. SMITH <

Approximately two years later, I went to the Social Security Administration and the Department of Motor Vehicles and my name has been officially changed back to my maiden name. Other than my borrowed name being on various legal papers – until all processes are complete – I am fully done with this part of my life…the part where I thought I was married for four and a half years and I have finally awakened from that nightmare.

The End for Now

Extras

Dear Reader:

Thank you for taking the time to read my true-life story.

As you were reading it I hope that you sensed that I was talking directly to you. Many times I get asked about the authenticity of this book and if these events really happened.

Please understand that the answer is undoubtedly YES! I did go through these situations. And I too was amazed at how many of the details I could remember.

God ordained this project so that I could help you.

I hope that based on my true-life experiences, you will be able to avoid some of these same situations in your life. Don't rush to get married…do your research…find out what is what…with and on the person you are contemplating marrying. Make sure that God says its time and pressures from life, family, friends, or society, are not forcing your decision.

Hopefully, I did not seem mad or bitter as you read this. I'm really not. Actually I am a truly whole and complete woman of God. Since the completion of my book, Vee has had another peace order filed in the Maryland Court system against him, so he hasn't allowed God to deliver him from his issues.

Although I have not seen my ex in years, I do know that if I did see him now, I would be able to hold my head up around him, because I never had a reason to feel less in myself worth or be ashamed. But more importantly, I am strong enough to say I forgive Vee (and really mean it) and I hope that you have sought forgiveness from God.

Throughout the duration of me living in Baltimore and writing my book, there have been many people who have come into my life, strengthened and encouraged me. I appreciate you all, but I don't want to start naming names because I may forget someone.

As you read this book, you may have been able to identify with one or more or my situations. Now you may need to keep your story in your mind to help someone else or write it down like I did. Don't let it condemn or hinder you. It's nothing to be ashamed of. But most of all make sure you can be Christ like and say I forgive you.

Mark 11:25 says, "And when you stand praying, if you hold anything against anyone, forgive him, so that your Father in heaven may forgive you your sins." In other words, if you can't forgive someone else then God can't forgive you.

If it is God's will for me to get married for real one day instead of going through a third *Thom Thumb* wedding, so be it. If not…well let's not think about that. I believe God is preparing Mr. Right in His Sight for me and I may end up writing a book about that marriage. God knows the desires of my heart.

Until then…

May the Lord watch between you and me while we are absent, one from another-Amen.

--*LaDonna*

Hidden…
But Not Lost

(Poems & Song Lyrics that God gave me to get me THROUGH the storms)

You

You've made a difference for me
When I needed somebody for me
Your turned my nights back to daytime
You've turned my sadness into happiness
You just don't know what you've done to me.

When I met you, I had no idea
What exactly was in store for me--
Happiness so unimaginable joy so irreplaceable
You made a difference in my life
You're the best thing that ever happened to me, for me.

You are my life, the love of my life
And you are mine, all mine; no other can ever come close
To take me away from what you have created
To take me away others may hate it

Who would have ever thought
God would allow you to be the love of my life?
Who would have ever thought
Time would allow love to come right on time?

I Don't Know Why...9/26/06

I don't know why
Every time I try to leave you alone
I hear your voice, you're still a thought in my mind?

I don't know why
Every time I try to move on
I'm pulled right back to you?

I can't explain
The hold that you have over me
I keep telling myself let him go
- I gotta move on

How can I move on in life
When you are still on my mind?
Am I afraid to live without you
After you have done me so wrong?

Everyone tells me to leave you alone
That you mean me no good
So why I am still attached to you-

Why can't I let go?

I Apologize

All I ever wanted
Was to have success in life
But as I went higher I didn't think about the price

I apologize for the pain that I caused you
I'm sorry for the time, the time we lost
Forgive me all I need is one more chance
To make it up to you

Money, women, cars, and clothes
Those materialistic things in life
That really weren't important
But they made me who I was

I apologize for the pain that I caused you
I'm sorry for the time, the time we lost
Forgive me all I need is one more chance
To make it up to you

Make it up to you
I wanna make it up to you

Inspired and written as an expression of an associates emotions while he was incarcerated.

(DDR aka Nell)

Lord I need you to move...

Lord I need you to move,
Help me feel your presence
Let me know it will be alright
If I keep you in my sight

Lord I need you to move,
Help me feel your presence
Let me know it will be alright
If I keep you in my sight

I need you to mo-oo-oo-oove Lord
mo-oo-oo-oove Lord
mo-oo-oo-oove Lord
I need you to mo-oove Lord

Come Home

I'm making a wish and I'm checking it twice
But is this really what I want
For you to stay gone
Night and day after day
Is this what I really want?

Oh how I wish that you would call
Oh how I wish that you would come over baby
Lets give it one more try baby
Tell me that it will be alright
Come home, come home, come home

A couple of hours if even a day
It seems like eternity
Since you went your way and I went mine
Its funny how time stands still

I need you home right next to me
This is where I-I know you belong
Let's give it one more try baby
Tell me that it will be alright
Come home, come home, come home

It's driving me crazy to think that you my baby wouldn't come on home to me.

Reignite My Fire

I miss you God, miss being in your presence.
I need you God, to return me to your presence.
I admit I let life's circumstances
Pull me away from you, now I need you Lord to

Reignite my fire Lord.

I want to praise you
I want to worship in your name
I need to praise you

Reignite my fire Lord

Holy Spirit, Holy Spirit
Oh Holy Spirit

Reignite my fire Lord

12 Principles of W.O.W (*being a Woman of Wonder*)
All scriptures came directly from www.bible.com

These are the foundations and principles to initiate and host a W.O.W. Help Meeting

I. **Have the desire to be free from the bondage of domestic violence YOU DO NOT HAVE TO SUFFER THROUGH THIS**.*(1 Thessalonians 5: 9-10 For God did not appoint us to suffer wrath (the anger of God) but to obtain salvation through our Lord Jesus Christ. one0He died for us so that, whether we are awake or asleep, we may live together with him*)

II. **A twelve week commitment is required.** You can get help and you will learn and grow. (*John 8:32 And ye shall know the truth, and the truth shall make you free*)

III. **Pray to God for yourself and the ministry.** (*Matthew 21:22 If you believe, you will receive whatever you ask for in prayer*)

IV. **Get a buddy in this program that you call and check on and who you feel comfortable sharing with, if you do not feel comfortable sharing in the group yet.** (*Galatians 6: 2 Carry each other's burdens, and in this way you will fulfill the law of Christ*)

V. **Bring your bible.** (*Deuteronomy 17:19 It is to be with him, and he is to read it all the days of his life so that he may learn to revere the LORD his God and follow carefully all the words of this law and these decrees*)

VI. **Be willing to share your experiences - someone else NEEDS to hear it.** (*John 8:33 They answered him, We be Abraham's seed, and were never in bondage to any man: how sayest thou, Ye shall be made free?*)

VII. **<u>Don't be afraid to ask for help – YOUR LIFE COULD DEPEND ON IT.</u>** (*2 Chronicles 20:4 And Judah gathered themselves together, to ask help of the LORD: even out of all the cities of Judah they came to seek the LORD*)

VIII. **<u>It is ok to show emotion.</u>** (*Psalm 126:5 Those who sow in tears will reap with songs of joy*)

IX. **<u>You can be free. Realize that you can survive, still be successful and still have a normal life.</u>** (*John 8:36 If the Son therefore shall make you free, ye shall be free indeed*)

X. **<u>You do not have to receive love through abuse.</u>** (*Ephesians 2:4-7 But because of his great love for us, God, who is rich in mercy, made us alive with Christ even when we were dead in transgressions—it is by grace you have been saved. And God raised us up with Christ and seated us with him in the heavenly realms in Christ Jesus, in order that in the coming ages he might show the incomparable riches of his grace, expressed in his kindness to us in Christ Jesus*)

XI. **<u>Protect yourself and your children</u>** (*Ephesians 1:11 Put on the whole armour of God, that ye may be able to stand against the wiles of the devil*)

XII. **<u>You already have the victory</u>**. (*1 Corinthians 15:57 But thanks be to God, which giveth us the victory through our Lord Jesus Christ*)

Do you have questions, comments, concerns or suggestions or simply want to reach LaDonna M. Smith?

Website:

http://www.ladonnamsmith.com

Email:

ladonna@ladonnamsmith.com

Myspace:

myspace.com/philatonianproductions

Facebook:

LaDonna M. Smith

Blackplanet:

Philatonianceo

Twitter:

philatonian

LaDonna strives to bring you the latest, most innovated and most effective products and services.

Therefore some of these sites are subject to change or be discontinued.

LaDonna M. Smith is available for:

Conferences

Workshops

Speaking Engagements

Author Panels & Discussions

Single's/Relationship Events

Book Readings & Signings

and more!

Please send an email with the subject "***Event Request***"
to info@ladonnamsmith.com

---

1 Corinthians 13: 4-10 (Message Bible Version)

Love never gives up.
Love cares more for others than for self.
Love doesn't want what it doesn't have.
Love doesn't strut,
Doesn't have a swelled head,
Doesn't force itself on others,
Isn't always "me first,"
Doesn't fly off the handle,
Doesn't keep score of the sins of others,
Doesn't revel when others grovel,
Takes pleasure in the flowering of truth,
Puts up with anything,
Trusts God always,
Always looks for the best,
Never looks back,
But keeps going to the end.

8 -10 Love never dies. Inspired speech will be over some day; praying in tongues will end; understanding will reach its limit. We know only a portion of the truth, and what we say about God is always incomplete. But when the Complete arrives, our incompletes will be canceled.

Love Doesn't Hurt!

www.ingramcontent.com/pod-product-compliance
Lightning Source LLC
LaVergne TN
LVHW010105170826
845678LV00012B/2253

* 9 7 8 1 4 5 0 7 2 0 3 6 6 *